The
TWELVE
DAYS
of
CHRISTMAS

For Dad
– L.C.

PUFFIN BOOKS

UK | USA | Canada | Ireland | Australia
India | New Zealand | South Africa

Puffin Books is part of the Penguin Random House
group of companies whose addresses can be found
at global.penguinrandomhouse.com.

www.penguin.co.uk www.puffin.co.uk www.ladybird.co.uk

First published 2016
This edition published 2019
001

Printed in China

A CIP catalogue record for this book is available from the British Library

ISBN: 978–0–241–40312–9

All correspondence to:
Puffin Books, Penguin Random House Children's
80 Strand, London WC2R 0RL

Supporting the world's leading museum of art and design,
the Victoria and Albert Museum, London

WILLIAM MORRIS

The TWELVE DAYS *of* CHRISTMAS

With illustrations by LIZ CATCHPOLE

LIST OF PLATES

William Morris artwork from the V&A archive

ABOUT THIS BOOK

The Victoria and Albert Museum has a long association with Christmas festivities. In 1843 its founding director, Henry Cole, sent the world's first Christmas card. Prince Albert, the museum's patron and founder, popularized in Britain the German custom of decorating a Christmas tree. Today, the museum continues this tradition by commissioning a well-known designer to decorate, or build, a Christmas tree for its galleries.

The traditional festive song 'The Twelve Days of Christmas', first appeared in the late eighteenth century. This special edition of the song is inspired by the V&A's collection of the work of Arts and Crafts pioneer William Morris.

Illustrator Liz Catchpole selected Morris patterns from the archive and introduced new artwork inspired by the collection to bring the words of the song to life. Catchpole's illustrations of birds and stylized foliage extend and interact with the original patterns to create beautifully realized scenes. They are closely inspired by Morris's work, and the cumulative words of the rhyme resonate with his repeat designs for wallpaper and fabrics. Morris was known for his mastery of colour, and the palette used in the book is inspired by his rich tones, with the addition of bright accents. Beautiful, striking and unique, this book is a stunning celebration of William Morris and is a true festive delight.

On the
FIRST day of
CHRISTMAS
my TRUE LOVE
gave to me...

A PARTRIDGE *in a* PEAR TREE

On the
SECOND
day of
CHRISTMAS
my TRUE LOVE
gave to
me...

TWO
TURTLE
DOVES

and a **PARTRIDGE**
in a **PEAR TREE**

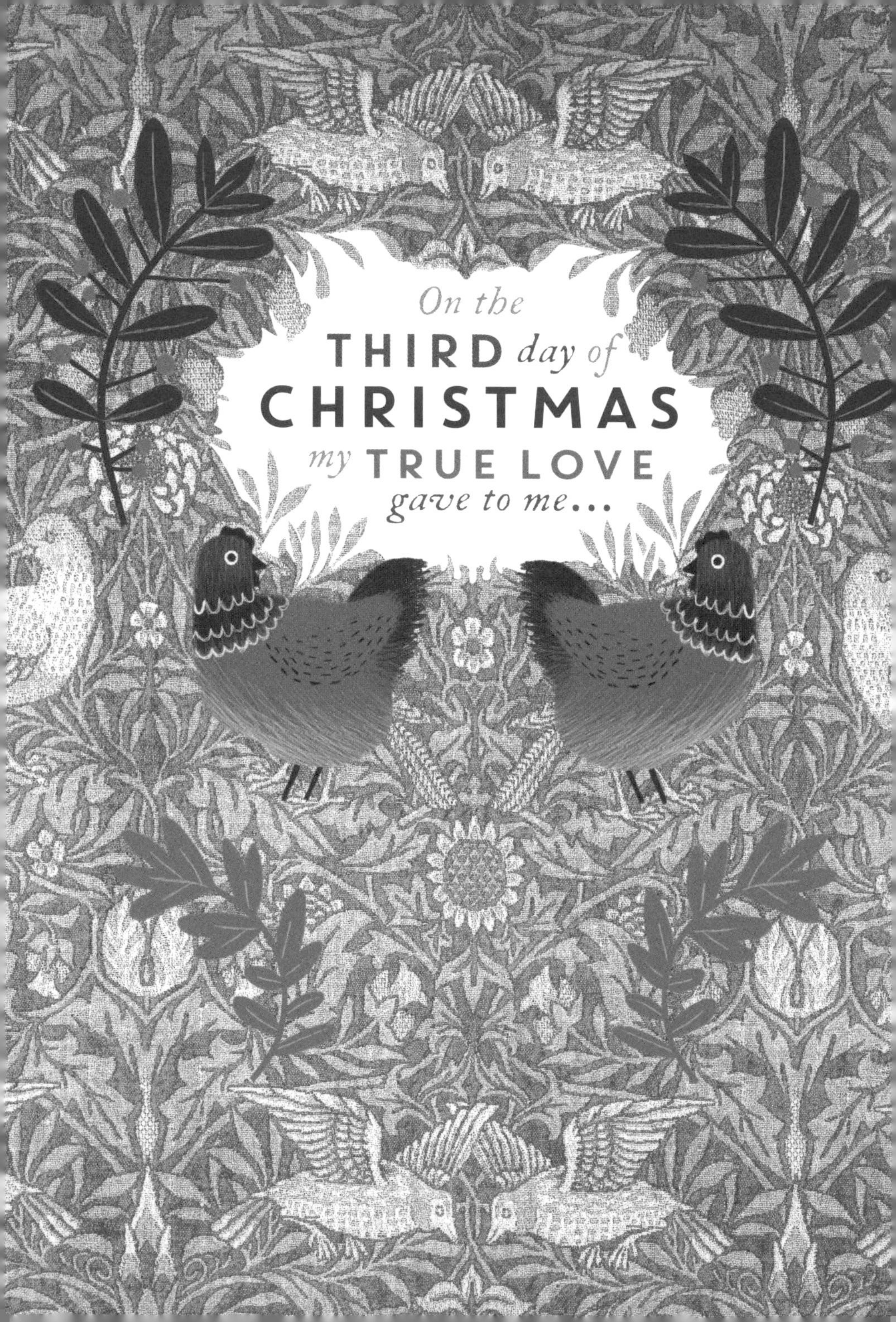
On the
THIRD day of
CHRISTMAS
my TRUE LOVE
gave to me...

THREE
FRENCH
HENS

TWO turtle doves

and a **PARTRIDGE**
in a **PEAR TREE**

On the
FOURTH day of
CHRISTMAS
my TRUE LOVE
gave to
me...

FOUR
CALLING
BIRDS

THREE French hens
TWO turtle doves

and a **PARTRIDGE**
in a **PEAR TREE**

On the
FIFTH day of
CHRISTMAS
my TRUE LOVE
gave to
me...

FIVE

GOLD RINGS...

...FOUR
CALLING
BIRDS

THREE
FRENCH
HENS

TWO
TURTLE
DOVES

and a
PARTRIDGE
in a PEAR TREE

On the
SIXTH day of
CHRISTMAS
my TRUE LOVE
gave to me...

SIX
GEESE
A-LAYING

FIVE gold rings
FOUR calling birds
THREE French hens
TWO turtle doves

and a **PARTRIDGE**
in a **PEAR TREE**

On the
SEVENTH day of
CHRISTMAS
my TRUE LOVE
gave to me...

SEVEN
SWANS
A-SWIMMING

SIX geese a-laying
FIVE gold rings
FOUR calling birds
THREE French hens
TWO turtle doves

and a **PARTRIDGE**
in a **PEAR TREE**

On the
EIGHTH day of
CHRISTMAS
my TRUE LOVE
gave to
me...

EIGHT
MAIDS
A-MILKING

SEVEN swans a-swimming
SIX geese a-laying
FIVE gold rings
FOUR calling birds
THREE French hens
TWO turtle doves

and a **PARTRIDGE**
in a **PEAR TREE**

On the
NINTH day of
CHRISTMAS
my TRUE LOVE
gave to me...

NINE
LADIES
DANCING

EIGHT maids a-milking
SEVEN swans a-swimming
SIX geese a-laying
FIVE gold rings
FOUR calling birds
THREE French hens
TWO turtle doves

and a **PARTRIDGE**
in a **PEAR TREE**

On the
TENTH day of
CHRISTMAS
my TRUE LOVE
gave to me...

TEN
LORDS A-LEAPING

NINE ladies dancing
EIGHT maids a-milking
SEVEN swans a-swimming
SIX geese a-laying
FIVE gold rings
FOUR calling birds
THREE French hens
TWO turtle doves

and a **PARTRIDGE**
in a **PEAR TREE**

On the
ELEVENTH
day of
CHRISTMAS
my TRUE LOVE
gave to
me...

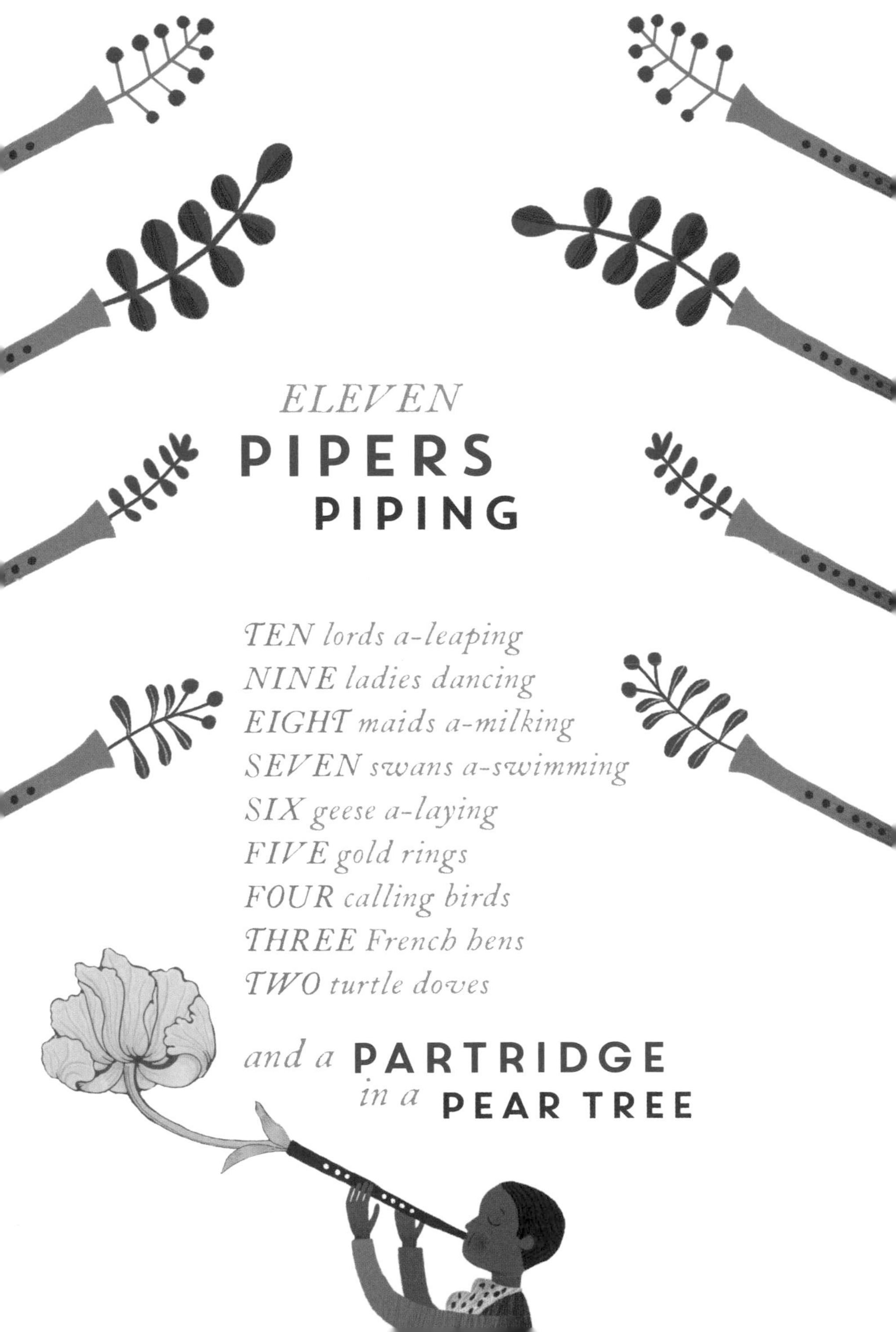

ELEVEN
PIPERS
PIPING

TEN lords a-leaping
NINE ladies dancing
EIGHT maids a-milking
SEVEN swans a-swimming
SIX geese a-laying
FIVE gold rings
FOUR calling birds
THREE French hens
TWO turtle doves

and a **PARTRIDGE**
in a **PEAR TREE**

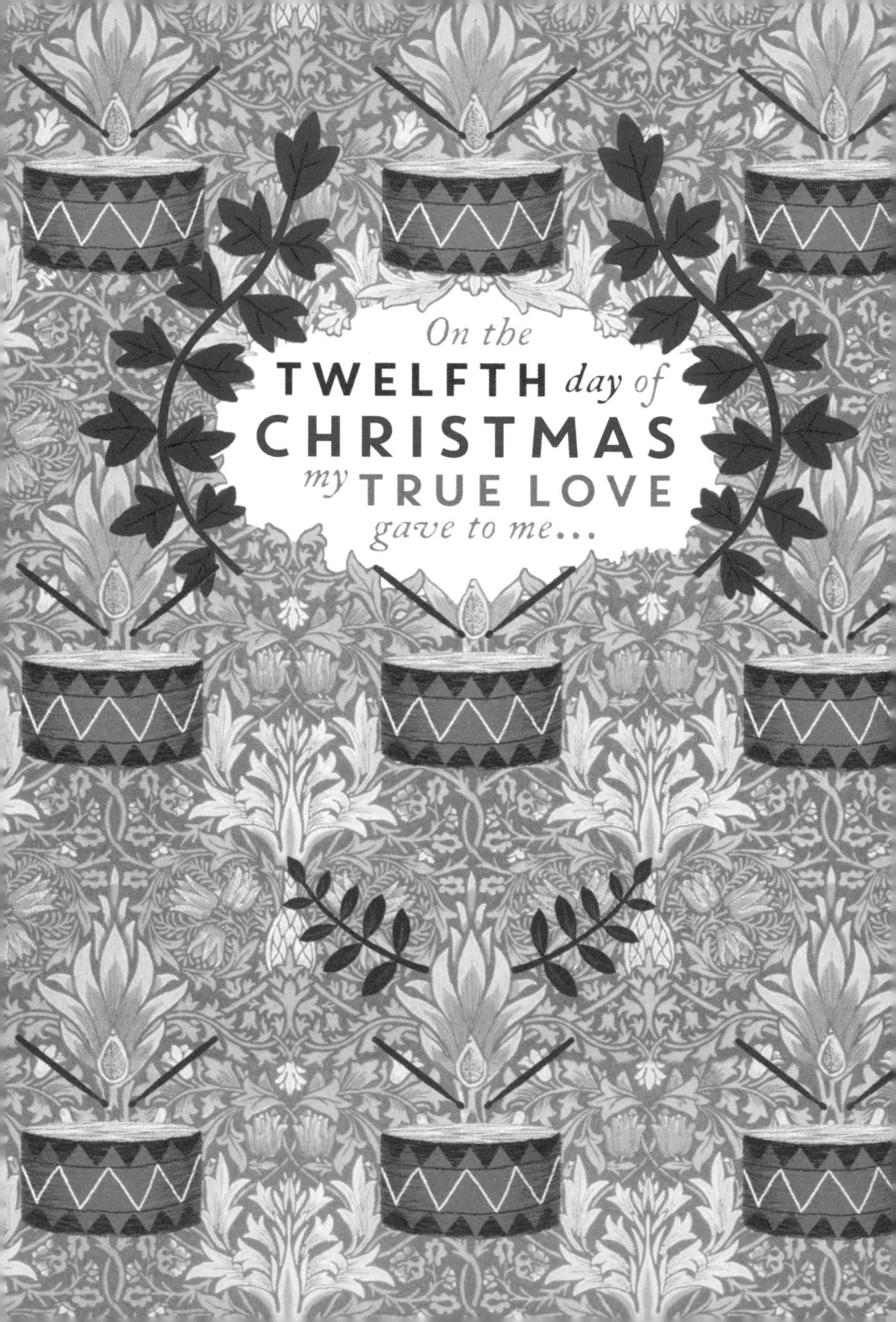
On the
TWELFTH day of
CHRISTMAS
my TRUE LOVE
gave to me...

TWELVE

DRUMMERS
DRUMMING

ELEVEN pipers piping
TEN lords a-leaping
NINE ladies dancing
EIGHT maids a-milking
SEVEN swans a-swimming
SIX geese a-laying
FIVE gold rings
FOUR calling birds
THREE French hens
TWO turtle doves

and a **PARTRIDGE**
in a **PEAR TREE**